The Gingerbread Man

Retold by Sally Bell

Illustrated by Jane Launchbury

A Golden Book • New York
Western Publishing Company, Inc., Racine, Wisconsin 53404

© 1990 Western Publishing Company, Inc. Illustrations © 1990 Jane Launchbury. All rights reserved. Printed in the U.S.A. No part of this book may be reproduced or copied in any form without written permission from the publisher. All trademarks are the property of Western Publishing Company, Inc. Library of Congress Catalog Card Number: 89-85576 ISBN: 0-307-11592-5/ISBN: 0-307-62592-3 (lib. bdg.)   A B C D E F G H I J K L M

A woman and a man
lived on a farm.
The woman said,
"I will make
a gingerbread man."
So she did.

Soon she heard something.
She looked.
The gingerbread man
jumped out.

The woman wanted to catch him.
The man wanted to catch him.
But the gingerbread man
ran away.

The gingerbread man ran fast.

He laughed.

He sang.

"Run, run, as fast as you can.

You can not catch me.

I am the gingerbread man!"

He saw a man.
The man was painting.
The man was painting
a house.

"Stop!" called the man.
"I want something to eat.
You look good."
The gingerbread man ran on.
The man ran after him.

The gingerbread man laughed.
He sang.
"Run, run, as fast as you can.
You can not catch me.
I am the gingerbread man!"

He saw a girl.
She was playing.
She had a ball.

"Stop!" called the girl.
"I want something to eat.
You look good."
The gingerbread man ran on.
The girl ran after him.

The gingerbread man laughed.
He sang.
"Run, run, as fast as you can.
You can not catch me.
I am the gingerbread man!"

He saw a boy.
The boy was riding.
"Stop!" called the boy.
"I want something to eat.
You look good."
The gingerbread man ran on.
The boy ran after him.

The gingerbread man laughed.
He sang.
"Run, run, as fast as you can.
You can not catch me.
I am the gingerbread man!"

The gingerbread man saw water.
He stopped.
He did not know what to do.
The gingerbread man saw a fox.
The fox saw him.

The gingerbread man sang.
"Run, run, as fast as you can.
You can not catch me.
I am the gingerbread man!"

The fox said, "I do not want
to catch you.
I will help you.
You can ride on me."

The gingerbread man got
on the fox.
The fox jumped into the water.
The fox said,
"You will get wet.
Ride on my head."
The gingerbread man did.

29

The fox said again,
"You will get wet.
Ride on my nose."
The gingerbread man did.
The fox put his head up.
The gingerbread man fell.

Snap!
The fox ate him up.
And that was the end
of the gingerbread man.